For family, friends, and especially Lila
— *R. K.*

With love, to my granddaughter Sierra
— *T. R.*

Henry Holt and Company, LLC
Publishers since 1866
115 West 18th Street
New York, New York 10011
www.henryholt.com

Henry Holt is a registered trademark of Henry Holt and Company, LLC
Text copyright © 2004 by Roberta Karim
Illustrations copyright © 2004 by Ted Rand
All rights reserved.
Distributed in Canada by H. B. Fenn and Company Ltd.

Library of Congress Catalog Card Number: 2003022496
Full Library of Congress Cataloging-in-Publication Data available at http://catalog.loc.gov/

ISBN 0-8050-6785-X / EAN 978-0-8050-6785-9
First Edition—2004
Designed by Amy Manzo Toth
Printed in the United States of America on acid-free paper. ∞

1 3 5 7 9 10 8 6 4 2

The artist used pencil, transparent watercolor, and some acrylic on
100 percent rag stock cold-press paper to create the illustrations for this book

Faraway Grandpa

by Roberta Karim

illustrated by Ted Rand

Henry Holt and Company / *New York*

*1*n a town far away
lived my Faraway Grandpa.
But when he wrote me a letter,
we were together!

North Main St.
June 1915

Dear Kathleen,
Heard a new song!
My old Irish heart sang along.
Write down the words
when you hear it.
We'll sing together this summer!
Oops, almost forgot.
The song is called "Danny Boy."
Such a fine name!
Love,
Grandpa Danny

*S*ummer filled the meadow.
I packed the words to our song.
Mum packed clothes.
Poppa hitched up Joe and Misty Rose.
Off we rattled to the faraway town
to visit my Faraway Grandpa.

Grandpa Danny loved shenanigans,
especially the Glasses Game.
He shouted to our wagon,
"What's your name, miss?"
"It's me, Grandpa!"
"Me, who? Can't see a thing without GLASSES!"
He pulled every pocket inside out, then bowed.
His glasses slid down his red polished head,
and landed *kerplunk* on his nose.
He leaped up. "Smithereens!
You're my granddaughter, the grand Kathleen!"

Neighbor Millie chuckled.
"That Danny. What a tease!"
Mum and Poppa ambled over to
her porch to jaw on news and toffee.

"Scorcher!" said Grandpa Danny.
He mopped his face and mine.
"But we can remedy that."

In his tall, cool kitchen
Gramps poured mugs of homemade root beer
with mountains of foam.
"So much foam," he whispered, "no one would
notice a scoop of my homemade ice cream,
now would they?"

We sat on the old porch swing.
My feet didn't reach the floorboards yet,
so Grandpa pushed off.
He thumped and thumped some more.
"I brought you the words to our song,"
I said. "Let's sing!"
"If you help me," he answered.
So we sang together:

> *"Oh Danny Boy, the pipes, the pipes are calling*
> *From glen to glen, and down the mountain side.*
> *The summer's gone, and all the roses falling.*
> *It's you, it's you must go and I must bide."*

Grandpa sang bass:

> *"But come ye back when summer's in the meadow,*
> *Or when the valley's hushed and white with snow."*

Grandpa's voice didn't reach the high notes,
so I had to finish loud and strong:

> *"It's I'll be here in sunshine or in shadow.*
> *Oh Danny Boy, oh Danny Boy, I love you so."*

About that time Millie went inside.
"She never listens long to our songs," I said.
Grandpa winked.
"'Tis only with her ears that she listens."
"What else would you listen with?" I asked.
He patted his chest. "The heart."

*T*wo weeks later our visit was over.
'Twas time for me to leave for home.
Gramps mopped his eyes with a hanky.
But I knew there would always be next year.

Next year,
when summer filled the meadow,
I wondered what to pack for our trip.
Gramps hadn't sent me a letter.

We rattled to the faraway town
to visit my Faraway Grandpa.
The roadside was vacant.
The tall house stood hushed.
"Where's Grandpa Danny?" I cried.
"We always visit August first," Mum said.
"Surely he remembered our coming!"
My heels hit the grass.

I found him around back.
"Kathleen?" said he, eyebrows popping.
"Don't call me Kathleen yet," I said,
eyebrows scrunched. "First we play the Glasses Game!"
"*I* don't wear glasses," said Gramps.
But then he said
"scorcher!" as usual.

Neighbor Millie clucked her tongue.
Mum and Poppa quick-footed over.
"That Danny," I heard Millie say.
"What a worry.
So many times he forgets."

Gramps and I walked hand
in hand to the kitchen.
He poured us root beer
with mountains of foam.
But the ice cream bucket
was empty.
"Did you forget to make
ice cream?" I asked.
"I forgot to remember,"
he said.

We sat on the old porch swing.
"Look, Gramps, my feet reach now!"
So *I* thumped and thumped some more.
"Do you remember our song?" I asked.
"Always," he said.
He pulled out my wrinkled paper,
and we sang like thunder.
Millie rubbed her ears and walked away.
"She never listens long," Gramps said.
"She listens with her ears," I said.
"What else would there be?" he asked me.
"The heart, Grandpa, the heart."
He jumped to his feet.
"That reminds me, Kathleen, come inside.
I've something to show you."

In the middle of sawdust stood a grand, handsome
dollhouse, curlycued just like Grandpa's home.
He tapped the tiny swing and grinned.
Two hearts were carved in the wood.
"That's for you and me," he said.

We stayed until fall in the faraway town.
And sometimes Grandpa forgot to remember.

Then one frosty morning
we hitched up Joe and Misty Rose.
The dollhouse sat between Gramps and me.
He was coming to live with us!
"Faraway Grandpa," I said,
"now you can change your name to Close."

My first year with Grandpa
kept me thinking.
In November,
Gramps hid eggs
in his sock drawer.

Was this a new game?
I hid peppermints in my toy box
to keep him company.

$\mathcal{I}$n February,
Gramps taught me riddles
he'd learned as a boy in Ireland.
I taught him riddles I'd learned yesterday.
"Funny, I don't remember yesterday," he said.
"I don't remember Ireland," I said.
He smiled. "We're good for each other."

In April, we played with the dollhouse every day.
Gramps thought he saw a girl in the kitchen.
So I said, "Scorcher! Let's pour her a root beer."
Then I tapped the porch swing and sang "Danny Boy."
"Kathleen, when you sing that song," he said,
"I listen with my heart."

*I*n July, Gramps forgot the rule about
picking Mrs. McConacky's marigolds.
"I'm so sorry," Poppa told her.
"I'm sure he won't do it again."

*S*o in August, Grandpa picked her petunias.
"Why can't Gramps remember?"
I asked Mum.
"A cloud is settling in his mind," she said.
"Some days will be shadowy;
some days will be clear."
"When it's shadowy," I said,
"I'll sing him our song."
"Perfect," said Mum.

*I*n November,
the first winter storm whirled
into the meadow.

Then the valley lay hushed and bright
with snow. From the sparkly blanket,
Mum and I stirred up a batch of
snow ice cream.
I carried a bowl to Grandpa's room.
But he was gone.

High and low we searched that day.
The snow had covered his footprints.
"Kathleen, you're cold," said Poppa.
"Go back to the house and wait."

I pulled off my mittens and boots,
my cloak and scarf,
and went to my room to cry.
My closet rustled. Once, twice.
Fearfully, carefully, I opened the door.

'Twas Gramps! Reading his wrinkled paper upside down.
"What's your name?" he asked.
"I'm Kathleen," I said. "Is this a shadowy day for you?"
The dollhouse sat on his lap.
He tapped the tiny porch swing and smiled.
"Wait right here!" I said.

"Gramps is found!"
I called to the meadow.

In the kitchen I sloshed root beer
in tall mugs, snow ice cream
in the foam.

I tugged Gramps over to the big rocking chair.
We sat side by side with our mugs.
"It's almost a porch," I said. "Let's swing!"
We tapped, then thumped and thumped some
more, slurping as we flew.

The root beer ran out.
The rocking chair stopped.
Gramps held up the wrinkled paper.
Softly I sang our song:

"... *I'll be here in sunshine or in shadow ...*"

And from far away . . .

my Grandpa Danny listened with his heart.

Danny Boy

Oh Danny Boy, the pipes, the pipes are calling

From glen to glen, and down the mountain side.

The summer's gone, and all the roses falling.

It's you, it's you must go and I must bide.

But come ye back when summer's in the meadow,

Or when the valley's hushed and white with snow.

It's I'll be here in sunshine or in shadow,

Oh Danny Boy, oh Danny Boy,

I love you so.

Danny Boy